DINOFOURS™

IT'S FIRE DRILL DAY!

To my sister, Lois
— S.M.

The editors would like to thank Judy Comoletti
of the National Fire Protection Association
for her expertise.

Text copyright © 1997 by Scholastic Inc.
Illustrations copyright © 1997 by Hans Wilhelm, Inc.
All rights reserved. Published by Scholastic Inc.
CARTWHEEL BOOKS and the CARTWHEEL BOOKS logo
are trademarks and/or registered trademarks of Scholastic Inc.

Library of Congress Cataloging-in-Publication Data

Metzger, Steve.
    It's fire drill day! / by Steve Metzger; illustrated by Hans Wilhelm.
        p.   cm. — (Dinofours)
    "Cartwheel books."
    Summary: Mrs. Dee, the preschool teacher, helps Albert overcome his fear of the loud noise of the fire bell by explaining that fire drills keep children safe. Includes fire safety tips.
    ISBN 0-590-37455-9
    [1. Fire drills—Fiction.   2. Fear—Fiction.   3. Nursery schools—Fiction.   4. Schools—Fiction.
5. Dinosaurs—Fiction.]
I. Wilhelm, Hans, 1945-   ill.   II. Title.   III. Series: Metzger, Steve. Dinofours.
PZ7.M56775Isf   1997
[E]—dc21   97-7316
                                                                                                                    CIP
                                                                                                                    AC

10 9 8 7 6 5 4 3 2 1

Printed in the U.S.A.   24
First printing, September 1997

DINOFOURS™
IT'S FIRE DRILL DAY!

by Steve Metzger
Illustrated by Hans Wilhelm

Cartwheel®
·B·O·O·K·S·

SCHOLASTIC INC.
New York Toronto London Auckland Sydney

Mrs. Dee and the children had just finished singing their "Good Morning" song on the rug.

"Today is a special day," Mrs. Dee said.

"Why?" asked Tara.

"We're going to have a fire drill," replied Mrs. Dee. "Does anyone know what that is?"

Tracy raised her hand. Mrs. Dee called on her.

"I know what it is, Mrs. Dee," said Tracy. "My big sister told me about the fire drill at her school. There isn't a real fire. The fire drill is just for practice. Everyone has to be quiet. All the children line up and go outside. Then everyone goes back inside."

"That's right," said Mrs. Dee. "It's important to have fire drills to make sure children know how to leave the school in a safe way—in case there ever *is* a real fire."

Suddenly, Brendan stood up.

"Look at me," he exclaimed. "I'm a firefighter, and I drive a big red fire truck!"

Brendan made the sound of a fire truck as he raced around the classroom. "Rrrrr! Rrrrr!"

"Please sit down, Brendan," said Mrs. Dee. "We're not finished."

Brendan plopped down between Joshua and Albert.

Albert raised his hand. Mrs. Dee called on him. "How will we know when the fire drill starts?" asked Albert.

"The fire bell will ring," said Mrs. Dee. "It will be very loud so everyone can hear it."

"When will it ring?" asked Albert, who now had a worried look on his face.

"Later, during our activity time," said Mrs. Dee. "I'll let everyone know just before it rings."

I don't like loud noises, thought Albert.

Circle time was over. As Albert was trying to decide where he wanted to play, he kept thinking about the fire bell.

Albert took his favorite doll and softly sang a song about how he felt:

I do not like the fire bell.
It's loud and hurts my ears.
I do not like the noise it makes.
I hope it disappears.

Joshua asked Albert to play with him in the blocks area. Together, they made a tall building by crisscrossing the blocks.

Albert wasn't having much fun. He was still thinking about the fire bell.

I can be louder than that silly bell, Albert said to himself.

Albert pushed over the block building. It fell down with a crash.

"What are you doing?" shouted Joshua.

"It's fun to make loud noises," said Albert. "Isn't it?"

"No, it's not!" Joshua stomped off. "You knocked the blocks down. You put them back."

Albert sadly put the blocks away by himself. Then he walked over to the shelf that held the musical instruments. He thought about the fire bell as he took down two cymbals.

Albert marched around the classroom, clanging his cymbals. The children looked up to see what was going on.

"Too loud!" they shouted. "Be quiet, Albert!"

Mrs. Dee helped Albert put away the cymbals and find a different activity. He picked the water table. Albert poured a bucket of water into the waterwheel. As he thought about the fire bell, he poured faster and faster.

The water splashed Tara. Albert shouted, "Splishy-splashy, splishy-splashy, loud, loud, loud!"

"Stop it, Albert!" cried Tara. "You're getting me all wet!"

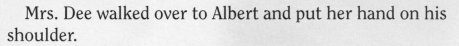

Mrs. Dee walked over to Albert and put her hand on his shoulder.

"Albert, what's going on?" asked Mrs. Dee. "I've never seen you act like this."

"I'm afraid of the fire bell," said Albert in a low voice. "I don't like loud noises." He was almost crying.

"I want to tell you something, Albert," said Mrs. Dee. "I don't like loud noises, either. But I *do* like the loud sound the fire bell makes."

"Why?" asked Albert.

"Because it's a sound that helps keep children safe. And that's my favorite kind of sound."

Albert smiled. Mrs. Dee looked up at the clock.

"Albert, it's time for the fire drill," she said.

"I'm ready," said Albert.

Then Mrs. Dee turned to face all the children.

"Children," said Mrs. Dee in a strong voice, "I need your attention. It's time for our fire drill."

Everyone stopped what he or she was doing.

Albert took a deep breath.

At that moment, the fire bell rang throughout the school. It made a loud, clanging sound.

That wasn't so bad, thought Albert.

Quickly and quietly, the children lined up in front of the door. Mrs. Dee led them outside. As the class walked down the road, Mrs. Dee counted the children to make sure they were all there.

They waited outside until Mrs. Dee told them to go back inside the school. They walked to their classroom and sat down together on the rug.

"That was a great fire drill, children," said Mrs. Dee. "Everybody left the school in a very safe way."

Just then, Albert got up and went over to the dress-up area. He put on a red firefighter's hat and sang a new song:

I like the fire bell.
I know I always will.
It tells us when to go outside
For our fire drill.

The Dinofours' Fire Safety Tips

• Be quiet during fire drills. It is important to hear what your teacher is saying.

• If a smoke detector sounds, get out of the house or building quickly. If there is smoke, crawl low under it on your way outside.

• Once you are outside, stay outside. Don't go back into a burning building for anyone or anything.

• Don't play with matches or lighters. If you find matches or lighters, tell a grown-up right away.

• Matches and lighters should be stored out of the reach of children, preferably in a locked cabinet.

• If your clothes catch on fire:

Stop where you are.

Drop to the ground and cover your face with your hands.

Roll over and over to put out the fire.

Remember: Stop, Drop, and Roll.

• Firefighters wear special equipment called breathing apparatus to help them breathe inside burning buildings. Although these masks might seem scary, don't hide from firefighters. A firefighter is there to help you.